THE
LITTLE LEAGUE TEAM
FROM THE
BLACK LAGOON

THE
LITTLE LEAGUE TEAM
FROM THE
BLACK LAGOON

GET OFF MY HEAD!

by Mike Thaler
Illustrated by Jared Lee

SCHOLASTIC INC.

New York   Toronto   London   Auckland   Sydney
Mexico City   New Delhi   Hong Kong   Buenos Aires

To Yonatan,
Who loves baseball—M.T.

To the good guys,
Rick, Doug, Brian and Larry—J.L.

Visit us at www.abdopublishing.com Reinforced library bound edition published in 2011 by Spotlight, a division of ABDO Publishing Group, 8000 West 78th Street, Edina, Minnesota 55439. This edition was reprinted by permission of Scholastic Inc. No part of this publication may be reprinted in whole or in part, or in any form or by any means, electronic or mechanical, without written permission of the publisher. For information regarding permission, write to Scholastic Inc., Attention: Permissions Department, 557 Broadway, New York, NY 10012.

Printed in the United States of America, Melrose Park, Illinois.
082010
012011

Library of Congress Cataloging-in-Publication Data
This title was previously cataloged with the following information:
Thaler, Mike, 1936-.
 The little league team from the black lagoon / by Mike Thaler ; illustrated by Jared Lee.
    p. cm. – (Black lagoon adventures ; #10)
 Summary: Hubie just feels sick because baseball fever is catching everyone. The only hit he had last year was when he got hit in the head by a ball. Will he make the big hit this year and knock the ball out of the park?
 [1. Baseball–Fiction.] I. Lee, Jared D., ill. II. Title.
 PZ7.T3 Lit 2007
 [E]–dc20   2007298222

ISBN: 978-1-59961-813-5 (reinforced library bound edition)

All Spotlight books have reinforced library binding and are
manufactured in the United States of America.

CONTENTS

BUG BOY →

WE NEED A HIT.

CHAPTER 1
TAKE ME OUT TO THE BALL GAME

It's baseball season. The sky is filled with little white balls, and the air with the swing of bats. All of my friends are pulling out their baseball gloves and pounding the pockets. I look for my mitt. It's not under my dresser. It's not under my bed. It's not in the refrigerator.

I finally find it in the corner of the garage. It's as stiff as a board. It's so old—it's prehistoric! It's a fossil. I feel like an archaeologist finding a dinosaur bone. I'd be

 ← BONE

better off using a paper plate or a pillow. But I put lots of oil on it and try to fold it around a ball. No way, it doesn't budge.

Little League tryouts are this Saturday. Freddy's got it made. He's the only one who wants to be catcher. Eric's got it easy . . . his dad's the coach. Derek's a slugger—he hit the only home run last year. Penny and Doris will make the team because they're *girls*. And Randy just wants to keep score and figure out everybody's statistics.

Last year, my batting average was zero. I walked twice, got hit by a pitch, and struck out ten times.

The only reason I played at all was they needed someone to stand in right field. They hoped no one would hit the ball out there. I hoped no one would, too.

You're out there all by yourself. You can hardly see the game. It gets lonely.

Then you hear the crack of the bat, and a little white missile sails out toward you. It's like a meteor falling from the sky. If you don't catch it, your team will lose the game.

You're out there all alone. Do you run in? Do you run back? Do you run to the left—do you run to the right?

You look up and are staring right into the sun. You can't see the ball at all. Then, all of a sudden, it drops on your head. The only one who is out . . . is you. When you wake up, you are surrounded by the team that lost . . . your team. They're glad you're okay so they can tell you, "*You* lost the game."

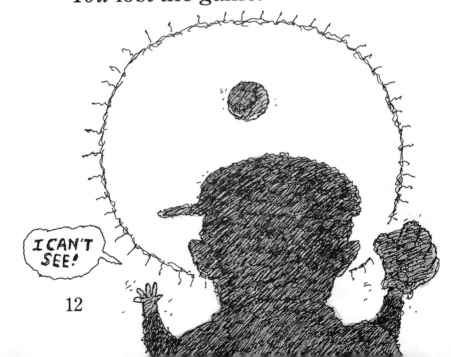

I CAN'T SEE!

CHAPTER 2
HAND IN GLOVE

This year I'm ready. I've been practicing. I play catch with Tailspin. I practice batting with a broom. I'll be able to sweep the bases, but I need a new mitt. Rigor mortis has set in my old one.

I ask Mom. I plead. I beg. She says okay, but I have to cut the lawn all year to pay for it. I say okay. I'm desperate.

We get in the van and drive to Sports World. They have all sorts of gloves lined up in a leather parade.

There are all kinds. Ones with one finger, ones with two fingers, ones with three fingers. I want one with five fingers. I need all the help I can get!

14

If the store had one with ten fingers, I'd get it. The bigger—the better. But they're all about the size of an apple pie. Some are signed by famous players. Others are just signed by a guy named Wilson. Never heard of him.

We finally find one that fits my hand and mom's pocketbook. I now have a new glove. It's like coming home with a new pet. It even smells like an animal.

15

The first thing I do is oil it and wrap it around a ball. Then I set it on my dresser overnight. We're going to be great friends. We're going to do great things. We're going to work together hand in glove. I fall asleep dreaming about my new baseball career.

OIL

RAG

GLOVE

MVP

CHAPTER 3
CATCH A FALLING STAR

It's the 9th inning. I'm standing in right field in a big ballpark. I hear the crack of the bat. I look up into the sky. No sun—it's a night game. The sky is full of stars—thousands of stars. Suddenly, one begins to fall. I have to catch it or we'll lose the game. It's falling fast. But a star has a long way to fall.

OH, NO!

Should I run forward? Should I run back? It looks like it's going to fall outside of the stadium. I run into the street. It's falling out of town. I run down the road. It's going to fall in the ocean. I get into a boat and row after it. But I can't row fast enough. The star splashes down in the water. Eight sharks in baseball caps surround my boat and shout out, "You lost the game!"

18

19

I wake up. My new mitt is still on the dresser. I inhale its aroma for reassurance ... *cowlogne* ... I'm ready. This season things are going to be different.

CHAPTER 4
GOT YA COVERED

I wear my mitt to breakfast. I've named it *Grabber*. It's a little hard to butter my toast, but I'm not taking it off. We're going to become one. We'll think as one, we'll move as one, we'll be one.

While I'm waiting for the school bus, I hit the pocket. No ball will escape my grasp. Grabber will grab anything that comes near us. Nothing will escape. I hold my schoolbooks in my mitt.

SMACK!
SMACK!

YOU HAVE LEGS.

YES, I'M SPECIAL.

When I get on the bus, T-Rex says, "Got a new mitt there, Hubie?"

"Its name is Wilson," I answer, "but I call it Grabber."

"Cool," says T-Rex, closing the door.

"Hey, you got a new mitt," exclaims Derek. "Let me try it on."

"No way," I say. "My hand will be the only one it will ever know."

"Welll!" declares Derek. "Fussy, fussy."

"Tryouts are tomorrow," states

WANT TO PLAY CATCH.

NO.

23

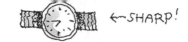

←SHARP!

Eric. "My dad says to be there at 10 a.m. . . . sharp. He says this year we're going to do better."

"That won't be hard," snickers Randy, "0-and-12 is not a tough record to beat."

"Let's hope that the other team won't show up to a game—so we'll have at least one win," says Penny.

HONK!

BEEP! BEEP!

HONK!

24

MITT　　MITTEN　　KITTEN

"That's not positive thinking," replies Eric.

"It's positively the truth," snorts Doris.

Why do girls always stick together? I just sit in the back and pound Grabber's pocket all the way to school.

CHAPTER 5
CLASS OF THE FIELD

"What happened to your hand?" asks Mrs. Green.

"He has baseball fever," says Freddy. "Your hand swells and you see stars."

"Can you hold a book?" asks Mrs. Green.

"Grabber can hold anything," I answer.

"Grabber!" chuckles Derek.

"Well, open to page 32," directs Mrs. Green. "Who was George Washington?"

I raise my hand with Grabber on it.

BASEBALL WITH A FEVER

27

CIRCLE THE
HOTDOG →

"Hubie," says Mrs. Green. "I see your hand is up."

"George Washington played 2nd base for the Cleveland Indians."

"No way," says Randy. "George Washington played 3rd base for the Boston Red Sox."

GEORGE WASHINGTON

THOMAS JEFFERSON

BASE

28

"Baseball fever," comments Penny with a knowing nod.

"All right," says Mrs. Green. "Who invented baseball?"

I wave my glove.

ANSWER ON PAGE 37.

29

"Yes, Hubie," sighs Mrs. Green.

"Abner *Doubleplay*," I answer.

"Abner Doubleday," corrects Eric.

"I like Abner Doubleplay better," I say.

←BASE   BALL→

"Well, my dad took me to Cooperstown and we spent a whole day in the Baseball Hall of Fame, and it's Doubleday," asserts Eric.

"Now, now," says Mrs. Green. "Who would like to tell us the history of baseball?"

BUG
↓

BUG
FOOD
↓

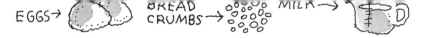

EGGS→ BREAD CRUMBS→ MILK→

My glove shoots up again.

"Hubie," groans Mrs. Green.

"Well, Abner Double*play* invented baseball at the dinner table. He was at home sitting in front of a plate. They were having chicken, and his wife was mixing up the batter to throw it in. There was also a pitcher of milk on the table.

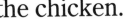

FLY

A fly flew on the table. Abner tried to hit the fly, but instead hit a ball of mashed potatoes which shot up into the air and landed on the chicken.

'It's a fowl ball,' declared Abner...and baseball was born."

All the kids sat there with their mouths open.

"Well," said Mrs. Green. "It's time for recess."

CRACK!

FOWL BALL!

CHAPTER 6
RECESSIVE GENES

CAPTAIN OF THE SEA →

TIRE PUMP ↓

"Let's play ball," I yell. I'm totally pumped.

"All right," says Eric, "I'll be captain and choose the teams."

"Why are you captain?" asks Penny.

"'Cause my dad's the coach," says Eric, folding his arms.

"Well, I want to be a captain, too," says Penny.

"Okay, okay, you can be a captain, too. Let's choose teams."

"I go first," declares Penny.

"Why do you go first?" asks Eric.

"'Cause I'm a girl," says Penny.

"Oh," says Eric.

ANSWER ON PAGE 44 →

BASEBALL IS PLAYED AT THE...
1. GLOVEPARK
2. BATPARK
3. BALLPARK

"I choose Doris," says Penny.
"I choose Derek," says Eric.
"I choose Randy," says Penny.
"I choose Freddy," says Eric.
"Who's left?" asks Penny. I wave my mitt. "Okay, I choose Hubie."

ANNOYING BARKING DOG →

37

ANSWER: RUN AROUND THE BASES.

"Ha," snickered Eric. "I have all the good players."

"We'll just see," says Penny. "We're up first."

"Because you're a girl?" asks Eric.

"Right," says Penny, grabbing the bat.

WHAT DOES A BASEBALL WEIGH? ① 3 oz. ② 5 oz. ③ 8 oz. ④ 12 oz.

ANSWER ON PAGE 43

Eric pitches the first ball high in the air. Penny swings and spins around.

"Strike one," grins Eric.

Penny brushes the hair out of her eyes. Eric rolls the ball on the ground. Penny swings.

"That's the old eye," taunts Eric. "Strike two."

BASEBALL FAN

← BASEBALL CAP

39

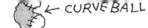 ← CURVE BALL

← SPIT BALL

Then Eric winds up and pretends to throw the ball—but doesn't. Penny swings.

"Strike three," shouts Eric, tossing the ball in the air. "You're out!"

"I get four strikes," demands Penny.

"Why?" asks Eric.

"Because she's a girl," sneers Derek.

THREE STRIKES, THAT'S ALL I GET?

LEFTOVER CHICKEN →

40

BAT →

CHAPTER 7
GOING BATTY

Everyone's pretty quiet on the bus home. Penny's not talking to Eric since he struck her out five times. Derek isn't talking to Penny because she took up all of recess at bat. Randy has started figuring out our stats, and I'm dreaming about when I'll be at bat. . . .

COOTIE (EXACT SIZE)

Z-Z-Z-Z...

BUS

A **DUGOUT** IS:
① A CANOE.
② YOUR FINGER IN YOUR NOSE.
③ A PLACE WHERE THE BATTING TEAM SITS.

ANSWER ON PAGE 46.

PITCHER'S
MOUND

The pitcher looks to the right, he looks to the left, he lifts his leg, he raises his arms, and he hurls the ball right over the plate. Strike one.

I shake the bat on my shoulder. I stare straight at him. He looks to the right . . . he looks to the left. He raises his leg, lifts his arms, and hurls the ball right at me.

42

I close my eyes and swing with all my might. Strike two.

Hey! Whose daydream is this anyway? It's not strike two—it's a hit!

I feel the bat connect, there's a loud crack, and the ball is sailing up into the air. It's going, it's going, it's gone. The fans go wild as I circle the bases.

← DIAMOND RING

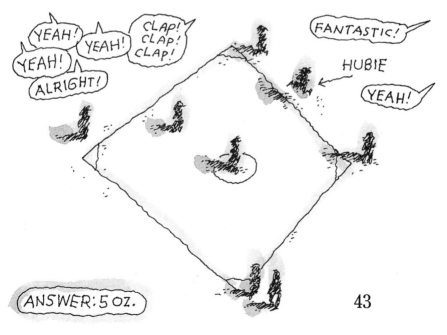

YEAH! YEAH! CLAP! CLAP! CLAP! YEAH! ALRIGHT! FANTASTIC! HUBIE YEAH!

ANSWER: 5 OZ.

43

"You're home," says Freddy, nudging me.

"I know," I answer, keeping my eyes closed.

ANSWER: BALLPARK

CHAPTER 8
HITS, RUNS, AND TERRORS

That evening, Grabber and I watch a baseball video together just to get in the mood. It's the life of Babe Ruth. He was the greatest hitter ever. He was so famous. They even named a candy bar after him. Maybe they'll name gumdrops after me—"Hubie Beans."

OH, NO!

← "THE BABE"

45

That night I have another dream. It's the final game of the World Series. It's the bottom of the 9th inning and the game is tied. There are two outs and I step into the batter's box.

46

But it's a real box. A big box and someone closes the lid. It's dark.

Outside, I hear "Strike one, strike two, strike three . . . you're out!" I hear all the fans booing. I never even saw the ball!

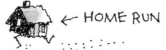

← HOME RUN

I wake up and my head's under my pillow.

It's Saturday. Time for tryouts!

WHAT SPORT IN THE UNITED STATES IS CALLED THE "NATIONAL PASTIME"?

(A) FOOTBALL
(B) BASKETBALL
(C) BASEBALL

ANSWER ON PAGE 50

← NORTH STAR

←HUBIE

CHAPTER 9
DIAMONDS ARE A BOY'S BEST FRIEND

STAR TREK

MOVIE STAR →

← STARFISH

I get to the ballpark early. No one's there. I stand at home plate and look out over the field. Soon this diamond will sparkle with the brilliance of my skills: batting, catching, running, jumping, skipping, hopping, and throwing. I'm going to be the most valuable player on the team. I'm going to be a star.

Eric and his dad arrive. Mr. Porter has a bag full of bats and balls. "Go out in the field, boys, and I'll hit you a few." Eric and I head out. Boy, it's a long walk.

"Here it comes!" shouts Mr. Porter. He hits a high fly ball.

"It's mine!" shouts Eric and he catches it.

"Good, son," says Mr. Porter. "Here comes another one . . ." *Crack*!

It's another high fly. "It's mine," shouts Eric, and he runs over and catches it.

"Good catch," shouts Mr. Porter and he hits another one. This is the highest one yet. It

BAG FULL OF BATS→

ANSWER: BASEBALL

CLOUD →

looks like its dropping out of a cloud.

"It's yours," I shout to Eric. He runs over, leaps up, and catches it. He winks at me and throws the ball back to his dad.

MISSILE →

"This one's for you, Hubie," says Mr. Porter.

"It's okay," I say. "I don't mind sharing."

"Here it comes, Hubie," says Mr. Porter, taking a tremendous swing that lifts the ball high into the sky.

I don't even see it for a while. Then I do. It's a tiny missile and it's heading straight for me. If I miss this one I'll never get another chance. I won't make the team. I may not even make the bench.

WHO STANDS BEHIND THE CATCHER?

(A) THE PRINCIPAL
(B) THE LIBRARIAN
(C) THE UMPIRE
(D) MOM

BATTER

CATCHER

ANSWER ON PAGE 58

← EGG, EASY UP.

It's dropping fast. I won't get a cap or a team T-shirt. I'll be the batboy or the water boy.

Should I run in? Should I run back? Should I run away?

It's headed straight for me and it's bringing the whole weight of the sky with it. I hold up Grabber and close my eyes . . . *Whomp!* It lands right in my pocket. I open my eyes, and there's a white ball resting in my glove like an egg in a nest. I take a deep breath, wink at Eric, and throw the ball back to his dad.

NEST

AFTER YOU GET A HIT AND YOU MAKE IT TO FIRST BASE, YOU ARE:
(A) LUCKY
(B) SWEATY
(C) TIRED
(D) SAFE

ANSWER ON PAGE 60

54

55

ANSWER ON PAGE 57

CHAPTER 10
A ROSE BY ANY OTHER NAME

"Well, what will we call our team this year?" asks Eric's dad.

"The Red Sox!" declares Randy.

"The White Sox!" insists Doris.

"The Smelly Sox!" laughs Eric.

"The Pantyhose," says Penny.

"The Firehose," jokes Eric.

"Hose on first?" asks Freddy.

"I don't know," says Penny.

"No, he's on third," laughs Derek.

SAFE AT FIRST →

ANSWER: BECOMES BATMAN

Anyway . . . an hour later we have our name. We're The Bobcats, since the coach's name is Bob, and we're his cool cats.

I'm glad his name isn't Jim, or our team name might be *The Jim Socks*.

THE MIGHTY BOBCAT

DANGEROUS TAIL

RADAR EARS

GRRRR!

SHARP CLAWS

POWERFUL LEGS

58

SCARY EYES

LONG TEETH

CHAPTER 11
THE REST IS HISTORY

Well, I make the team. I get the cap and the T-shirt. Since I'm not so tall, Mr. Porter tells me to play shortstop. You get to stand in the infield and it's not so lonely. Eric plays second base and Derek plays third. We can talk and tell jokes throughout the whole game.

59

The ball doesn't come high in the air. It's usually rolling on the ground. That's a lot easier. There's always someone behind you if you miss it. I just have to scoop it up and throw it to first base.

Mr. Porter says I have a good arm. I even made a double play during the last game. I flipped the ball to Eric and he threw it to first. He has a good arm, too. I'm proud of all of our arms. I'm proud of our whole team.

We're doing better this year. Our record is 3-and-3 so far.

ANSWER ON PAGE 62

I even got a hit and made it to first base. Mom told me never to be dishonest, but I stole second anyway. Then Derek hit a double, and I ran home and scored.

Everyone cheered. Mom clapped. And Tailspin wagged his tail.

ANSWER ON PAGE 64

What a wonderful feeling it was crossing home plate, and seeing the numbers change on the scoreboard.

I felt important, like I really added something to my team.

Like I'm real.

Like I count.

Like I'm a baseball player.

I DID IT!

BOBCATS 4
SALMONS 3

BOBCATS

ARF!
ARF!
ARF!

BASEBALL TRADING CARD

BOBCATS

STATISTICS

NAME: HUBIE • FAVORITE FOOD: PIZZA
TEAM: BOBCATS • HOBBY: DAYDREAMING
POSITION: SHORTSTOP • HERO: BABE RUTH

ANSWER: GRABBER